Sid Fleischman

The Library of Author Biographies™

Sid Fleischman

Jeri Freedman

rosen central™

The Rosen Publishing Group, Inc., New York

To my niece and nephew, Laura and Matthew Freedman, with love

Published in 2004 by The Rosen Publishing Group, Inc.
29 East 21st Street, New York, NY 10010

Copyright © 2004 by The Rosen Publishing Group, Inc.

First Edition

All rights reserved. No part of this book may be reproduced in any form without permission in writing from the publisher, except by a reviewer.

Library of Congress Cataloging-in-Publication Data

Freedman, Jeri.
Sid Fleischman / Jeri Freedman.— 1st ed.
 p. cm. — (The library of author biographies)
Summary: Discusses the life and work of this popular author, including his writing process and methods, inspirations, a critical discussion of his books, biographical timeline, and awards.
Includes bibliographical references and index.
ISBN 0-8239-4019-5 (library binding)
1. Fleischman, Sid, 1920– —Juvenile literature. 2. Authors, American—20th century—Biography—Juvenile literature. 3. Children's stories—Authorship—Juvenile literature. [1. Fleischman, Sid, 1920– 2. Authors, American. 3. Authorship.] I. Title. II. Series.
PS3556.L42269Z66 2004
813'.54—dc21
                                                                 2003005203

Manufactured in the United States of America

Material from "Sid Fleischman" by Paul Fleischman. *The Horn Book Magazine*, July/August 1987, pp. 429–430. Used with permission of the author.

Text from Sid Fleischman's "Newbery Medal Acceptance" for *The Whipping Boy*, reprinted in *The Horn Book Magazine*, © 1987 by Sid Fleischman. Used by permission of the author.

Text from *The Ghost on Saturday Night*, © 1997 by Sid Fleischman. Used by permission of HarperCollins Publishers.

Text from *The Ghost in the Noonday Sun*, by Sid Fleischman. Used by permission of HarperCollins Publishers.

Text from *St. James Guide to Children's Writers*, 5th ed. St. James Press, © 1999, St. James. Reprinted by permission of The Gale Group.

Text from *Mr. Mysterious & Company*, by Sid Fleischman. Used by permission of HarperCollins Publishers.

Text from *The Whipping Boy*, by Sid Fleischman, © 1986 by Sid Fleischman. Used by permission of HarperCollins Publishers.

Table of Contents

Introduction: The Magic of the Past		7
1.	Birth of a Magician	11
2.	Taking It on the Road	16
3.	The War and Its Aftermath	24
4.	New Wonders	35
5.	Lost Boys and Found Treasure	48
6.	Spoiled Brats and Noble Waifs	57
7.	The Art of Writing	62
	Interview with Sid Fleischman	69
	Timeline	73
	Selected Reviews from *School Library Journal*	77
	List of Selected Works	83
	List of Selected Awards	87
	Glossary	90
	For More Information	94
	For Further Reading	95
	Bibliography	97
	Source Notes	101
	Index	106

Introduction: The Magic of the Past

Sid Fleischman was surprised at the turn his life took when he became a writer. In the speech he gave when he won the prestigious Newbery Medal in 1987 for his book *The Whipping Boy*, he had this to say: "It never occurred to me to become a writer. First, my fingers got tired. And I had never seen a live author. They seemed as remote and mysterious and invisible as phantoms. I subscribed to the childhood folklore that all authors are dead. Or ought to be."[1]

From the time Sid Fleischman was a boy, his ambition was to be a magician, and the first book he wrote (when he was only seventeen years old) was about how to perform sleight-of-hand tricks. Fleischman's very first children's book, *Mr. Mysterious & Company* (1962), was written for his own children, and when they were young, he read to them from the books he was working on. After his father won the Newbery Medal in 1987, Paul Fleischman talked about what it was like to listen to his dad's works in progress. As he said:

> I'd be dimly aware that my father had been typing. His study door would open and close. My mother would call my two sisters and me, the whole family gathering in the living room, my father always at the table in the corner. Everyone got comfortable . . . A brief recap of the story was given. Then he read aloud the chapter he'd just finished . . . We were transported at once to the Old Post Road, to the decks of an Ohio River raft, to Hangtown or Matamoros. Part yarn-spinning session, vaudeville act, history lesson, and magic show, these readings transmitted, aside from their stories, so much of what I associate with my father.[2]

Sid Fleischman's stories are frequently set in the Midwest or in the Old West. Most often, they take place in the past. For example, *The 13th Floor: A Ghost Story* (1995) is set in New

England in the 1600s, and *By the Great Horn Spoon!* (1963) takes place during the California gold rush of the 1800s. Whatever the setting of Fleischman's stories, you can be sure that they will be exciting and adventurous.

Fleischman's main characters, young teenagers, often find themselves on a quest—to find a parent, a treasure, or a better way of life. In telling the stories of these characters, he taps into some of the most basic desires we all share—the need for security, a family, and a place to call one's own. At the same time, Fleischman's stories are funny. For instance, in *The Whipping Boy* (1986), a young prince finds himself a prisoner of a villain who smells so bad that he's nicknamed Hold-Your-Nose Billy.

Sometimes the characters find themselves in situations that are unexpected, if not downright bizarre. One example is what happens to Praiseworthy in *By the Great Horn Spoon!* The middle of the California gold rush is an unusual place to find a proper English butler like Praiseworthy. But he loyally accompanies his employer's young nephew to California, and the skills he has learned as a butler help them survive the many challenges they encounter on the voyage and in the goldfields. Even odder are the experiences of farmer Josh McBroom, who finds an acre of soil where a cornstalk grows as big as a tree. In *McBroom's Wonderful One-Acre Farm* (1982), McBroom must deal with the usual problems like his evil neighbor's attempt to force him to give up his land by sowing seeds that grow into giant weeds.

Fleischman's characters are quite often resourceful and clever. For example, Liz, in *The 13th Floor* (1995), is a young lawyer who finds herself arguing a court case back in 1600s New England, the time of the Pilgrims. Then there is Oliver Finch, who with the help of a couple of "good" pirates, convinces Captain Scratch (the wicked pirate captain) that he's dead, in *The Ghost in the Noonday Sun* (1965). And, of course, being a magician, Sid Fleischman doesn't hesitate to use magic when necessary. In *The Midnight Horse* (1990), an orphan boy named Touch enlists the help of a magic man to foil his great-uncle Judge Wigglesforth, who is trying to cheat him out of his inheritance.

If you're wondering how a young magician was transformed into a writer who draws his readers into the past with the magic of words, read on.

1 Birth of a Magician

Sid Fleischman was born in Brooklyn, New York, on March 16, 1920—an era as different from today as the settings of his stories. His full name is Albert Sidney Fleischman, but he was called Sid at home. When he was seven or eight, his mother told him that his real first name was Albert. He hated the name and continued to call himself Sid. Sid Fleischman's father, a Jewish immigrant from Russia, came to New York in 1908. His mother was the daughter of Jewish immigrants who went to England from Russia and Lithuania, and later immigrated to the United States in the late nineteenth century. Sid has two sisters—an older sister named Pearl and a younger one named Honey.

New York in the 1920s was a city on the verge of the modern age. Horse carts were being replaced with automobiles, the subway extended to Coney Island, and women had just won the right to vote. By the 1920s, Sid's father, Reuben, was fed up with the working conditions in the sweatshop factories where he was a tailor, and turned to other occupations. His jobs ranged from driving a taxi to being a shop-keeper, an occupation he wasn't very good at. When Sid was two, his father went to San Diego. Shortly thereafter, Reuben Fleischman moved his whole family across the country by train to a new home in California.

Something Magic in the Air

In the 1920s, the Fleischmans became owners of what was then a wonderful new entertainment device—the radio. It may be hard to imagine radio being thrilling, but in the 1920s, it was as important a form of entertainment as television is today. At the time, music and stories were told in serial form in radio broadcasts. In a serial, a story is told in weekly episodes. It was in one of these serials that young Sid encountered Chandu the

Magician. Chandu the Magician, the hero of the show, traveled all over the world fighting villains with his magic powers. Sid was enchanted by Chandu. It was the beginning of his love for magic, which is still a feature in his writing.

In the 1930s, following the stock market crash of October 1929, the United States fell into the Great Depression. By 1932, between 11 and 12 million people had lost their jobs, and many of those who remained employed made less money than they used to.

Despite the harsh conditions of the times, Sid Fleischman's thoughts were on magic. His dream was to be a magician, and he pursued this goal with single-minded intensity. He read volumes on magic, devouring famous books on performing card tricks and other types of magic that required only small objects such as coins.

Fleischman recounted his childhood pursuit of magic in his Newbery Medal speech:

> My search for secrets led me straight to the public libraries. I'd make a beeline to the shelves where the magic books sat. I hopped streetcars to the outlying branches. I'd take the nickel ferry across the bay to Coronado to check the shelves there . . . I taught myself sleight of hand out of library books.[1]

The Mirthful Conjurers

Sid was fourteen and in junior high school when he saw a write-up in a San Diego newspaper describing the Magicians' Club of San Diego, a group of magicians who met regularly to develop new tricks and try them out on each other. Sid went to the address given in the article and met the president of the club, Charles W. Fait, also known as Professor Fait the Great—a retired magician who for thirty-three years had had a traveling magic show that performed throughout the Midwest.

Through the magic club, Sid met Buddy Ryan, a fifteen-year-old who'd recently come to San Diego from Whitefish, Montana. The boys showed each other magic tricks and came up with new ones. They practiced on Sid's sisters, Pearl and Honey, and on Buddy's older sister, Mary, who would eventually join them as a magician's assistant.

The magic club gave the boys the chance to work up new tricks and practice performing. Before long, they started performing magic shows around San Diego. Calling themselves the Mirthful Conjurers, they charged a total of $2.50 (equal to about $50 today) for a forty-five minute performance, and they performed sleight-of-hand tricks with colored handkerchiefs, ropes, and balls.

In the summer of 1936, when Sid was sixteen, he and Buddy decided to take their magic show on the road during summer vacation from school. Because they needed transportation for their road trip, Sid took a job at a grocery store to earn his share of the $35 required to buy an old Essex automobile. At the time, it cost about $700 to buy a new car.

Summer came and Sid and Buddy loaded up the car with suitcases, magic props, and handbills (sheets of paper advertising the show that were passed out to people) that Sid had run off in the school shop. Then, Sid, Buddy, Mary, and Mary's German shepherd, Pal, set out for Lake Tahoe to find show-business success.

2 Taking It on the Road

The only definite booking Sid and Buddy had for their show, called See'n Is Believ'n, was at the Emerald Bay Camp in the Sierra Nevada of California. On their trip through the mountains, they stopped at such places as civilian conservation camps, which President Franklin Roosevelt's administration had created in the wake of the Depression. At these camps, the U.S. government paid unemployed young men and teenagers to perform work such as clearing land and building roads, which allowed them to earn money while doing useful work for the country. These men welcomed entertainment and were happy to pay the $5 fee that was charged for the magic show.

According to Fleischman, the humor in the magic show wasn't always subtle. As he said about one trick, "We'd invite several people onstage and pour them free drinks from a black bottle, then break the glass and show the white rat inside. We promised mirth [laughter], didn't we?"[1]

An Author Is Born

The magic road show would prove to be very influential. Aside from the trip giving Sid a sense of what it was like to journey around the country, it fed his craving to be a magician and, most important, led to his first writing effort. In addition, the rugged mountain towns and the gold country of California would later appear as settings in some of his books.

Sid had started to invent new magic tricks, and this led him to want to share his new creations. He was in his last year of high school when he wrote his first book, *Between Cocktails* (1939), and naturally, it was about magic. He wrote the short book on an old Remington typewriter, and for the illustrations, his uncle Sam took pictures of Sid's hands as he performed the tricks. The book explained how to do tricks with matches—tricks that could be done informally, while people were having cocktails, for example. Fleischman once said this about his first book: "In literary style, it was on a par with [similar to] the instructions you get with a digital clock."[2] However, he notes that the book has never been out of print.

Vaudeville and Spook Shows

Having completed high school, Sid was faced with the need to find a way to support himself. Although he came from a long line of tailors, he couldn't sew at all. But he could do magic tricks, so he set out to try his luck as a professional magician. In the pre–World War II United States, vaudeville theaters were still a common form of entertainment. Vaudeville was a live variety show in which various performers sang, danced, and put on funny skits, comedy routines, and animal acts. They also did magic. There were vaudeville theaters throughout the United States, in both large cities and small towns. Performers would travel from theater to theater, putting on their acts.

In search of success, Sid left San Diego and went to stay with his Uncle Sam and Aunt Pearl, who lived in Alhambra, a town near Los Angeles. He made his debut at a rundown vaudeville house in L.A. called the Hippodrome Theater, where he was paid $15 per week (equal to about $250 per week today) for performing five shows per day, three days a week. From there he moved on to small neighborhood theaters.

Then one day, he heard from his old friend Buddy, who had been traveling as a stage assistant with a spook show. Spook shows, scary shows featuring zany magic tricks and illusions, were performed in movie theaters after the last movie was shown. These shows provided a way for Depression-era theater owners to earn extra money by selling tickets to another show after the last movie. Some theater owners made more money from the spook shows than from the regular films they showed.

Buddy wanted to return to California and suggested that Sid replace him in the Francisco Spook and Magic show. For his work as a magician's assistant, Sid was paid $4 per show the first year he was with the show. His pay was increased to $6 per show the second year, a fee that was considered extremely generous by Depression standards.

In his autobiography, Fleischman describes what it was like to travel with Francisco's spook show:

> For the next two years, I was in a different town almost every night, largely in the Midwest. There I stumbled across the story address [location] for several novels and particularly the McBroom tall tales.
>
> The spook show was in perpetual [constant] motion, playing one-night stands in small-town movie theaters. Francisco, the ghost raiser, was a six-foot gentlemanly graying magician. As one of two stage assistants, I wore a red jacket with brass buttons.
>
> The spook show swung open its curtains at midnight, bringing forth phosphorescent [glow-in-the-dark] bats and glowing goblins for the last ten minutes of what was essentially a program of off-the-rack magic tricks.[3]

Echoes of Sid's spook show experiences can be clearly seen in Professor Pepper's ghost-raising show in *The Ghost on Saturday Night* (1974), in which the professor promises to raise the ghost of Crookneck John, a hanged outlaw.

While traveling with the spook show in the Midwest, Sid was exposed to many different dialects. People had different accents and interesting sayings. And when Sid began to write stories, he often used these colorful expressions and unusual names.

First Steps and Missteps

In 1939, while he was traveling with the spook show, *Between Cocktails* came out. According to Sid, seeing his name on the cover of a book "was like having one's name in lights."[4] Thrilled by having had a book published, he wanted to write more and see that work in print, too. His first attempts to write short stories, however, showed him that it wasn't easy. He thought that getting a better education would help him with his writing, and he decided to go to college.

In order to pay for his college fees, he came up with the idea of inventing magic tricks and selling them for $1 each in magic magazines. After coming up with a name for this venture, the Little Shop of Hocus Pocus, Sid went into business. As he describes it, the small business consisted of "a card table in [his] bedroom at home in San Diego."[5] Sid invented tricks while he was on the road, and he sent home the instructions for performing them. At home, his mother filled the orders that came in, and Sid earned enough to pay for his college tuition.

Once he had his money, he quit the spook show to enroll in San Diego State College, now

San Diego State University. To cover additional expenses while taking classes, he supplemented his income by performing magic at local nightclubs. Though the college didn't have a fiction-writing program, Sid learned as much as possible from the literature and other courses that were offered. And just like he had learned how to be a magician, Sid hunted the library, this time in search of specific knowledge on how to become a writer.

At San Diego State, Sid came across a teacher, John Adams, who was very helpful. Adams taught him how to appreciate literature and encouraged him to write. As Sid recalls, "In those days, I was no literary diamond in the rough—I wasn't even a zircon [glass that looks like diamond]—but Dr. Adams seemed to take my aspirations seriously."[6]

A life-changing experience happened to Sid Fleischman while he was in college. He met Betty Taylor, "a slim girl in a pink angora sweater and saddle shoes . . . a Spanish-language major with watercolor green eyes."[7] College and romance were soon to be interrupted, however. At 7:53 AM on December 7, 1941, the Japanese launched an attack on Pearl Harbor, Hawaii. The attack sank or damaged eight battleships and destroyed half a dozen other naval vessels and 188 aircraft. The next day, the United States declared war on Japan and entered into World War II.

3 The War and Its Aftermath

Sid Fleischman was a member of the naval reserve, which consists of people who train in the military part-time and are available for active duty in case of emergency. Within a couple of days of the bombing of Pearl Harbor, Fleischman was called up for duty. In the wake of the Japanese attack, volunteers rushed to join the U.S. armed forces. Recruiting centers were overwhelmed, and the military was faced with processing enormous quantities of paperwork. When Fleischman reported to the navy and they realized that he was a good typist, he was immediately given a petty officer's rank of yeoman third class and was sent into the recruiting service to do administrative work.

Serving in the Pacific

Sid and Betty married in 1942. Sid also continued to write short stories. Eventually, he sold a story to *Liberty*, a popular magazine of the day, for $250. Shortly after this triumph, however, he received word that he was to report to Norfolk, Virginia, to ship out. Fleischman served on the USS *Albert T. Harris*, a newly completed destroyer escort designed as a submarine hunter. As their name implies, destroyer escorts accompanied and protected convoys (groups) of supply ships, which were too lightly armed to protect themselves in enemy waters. Fleischman's love of the sea and ships provided the setting for two of his novels.

The hero of *The Ghost in the Noonday Sun* is the son of a Nantucket, Massachusetts, sailor, who finds himself kidnapped and taken to sea on a pirate ship. Much of the action in *The 13th Floor* also takes place aboard a pirate ship, this time in the seventeenth century. When the main character, twelve-year-old Buddy, travels into the past, he finds he must learn to handle himself on the ship quickly if he wants to survive. And this is not an easy task for a modern boy.

Fleischman's writing experience came into play onboard the USS *Albert T. Harris*, where among his other responsibilities, he edited the ship's newspaper. His main duty, however, was to be the captain's talker—someone who receives reports from the various parts of the ship and transmits the captain's orders.

The USS *Albert T. Harris* participated in two attacks in the Philippines and in the invasion of Brunei, a small country in the South China Sea, located on the northwest coast of Borneo. Toward the end of the war, the ship was stationed in Samar Bay in the Philippines. There and in nearby Leyte Gulf, also in the Philippines, the Pacific Fleet was gathering for a huge attack on Japan. As Fleischman recalled, the military "expected casualties to run a million and a half of us farm boys and city slickers. Japanese casualties were figured at ten to fifteen million. The invasion of Japan would be a bloodbath."[1]

On August 6, 1945, the United States dropped atomic bombs on the Japanese cities of Hiroshima and Nagasaki. Within a week, the Japanese surrendered, ending the war in the Pacific. Instead of going home, however, the

USS *Albert T. Harris* was sent to China, and Fleischman found himself in Shanghai, a large city on the eastern coast of mainland China. (He would later draw on his experiences here for his book *Blood Alley*.)

Life After the War

After his return to San Diego, Sid and Betty moved into a one-bedroom house that rented for $21 a month. He decided to try his luck as a full-time writer, while Betty supported them by working at the Veterans Administration. Although he wrote short story after short story as fast as he could, only a few were picked up for publication.

Then one day, Fleischman discovered Raymond Chandler, the author of famous private eye novels such as *The Big Sleep* (1939), and he was inspired to try his hand at writing a detective story featuring a murder. Of his early attempts at novel writing, Fleischman says, "I had read in one of the trade magazines that a professional should be able to write twenty pages a day, and I believed it."[2] He wrote his first full-length novel as fast as possible. However, when writing at such a quick pace, he wasn't able to pay enough attention to the details, and when the book was done it was terrible, forcing him to go through a long and dull process of rewriting. After that experience, he decided to approach writing his own way rather than by following what the "experts" said.

However, he did learn something useful from writing this first book. As he neared the end of the book, Fleischman realized that he didn't know who had committed the murder. He eventually figured it out, but the importance of this realization was that, "It gave [him] the brash confidence to start a novel without knowing the ending." As he says, "In all the years and books since, I've never lost a novel because I couldn't figure out how to tie things up for the final curtain."[3]

He called his first novel *The Straw Donkey Case* (1948). The title comes from one of the clues in the detective story—a straw donkey that is commonly sold in Tijuana, Mexico. Despite its awkward beginnings, *The Straw Donkey Case* did find its way into print. It was published by a small publishing company, Phoenix Press, in 1948, and Fleischman was paid an advance of $150. Within a year, Phoenix Press also bought a second detective novel from Fleischman and paid another $150 advance. Eventually, Fleischman should have received additional payment in the form of royalties for his two books. Unfortunately, Phoenix Press never paid the promised royalties, and the company eventually went out of business.

Short Stories and Front Pages

In the late 1940s, the government subsidized (provided money for) veterans who wanted to go to college, and Fleischman took advantage of this opportunity, returning to San Diego State College. There he took a course in short stories, taught by William Brunner. Prior to becoming a teacher, Mr. Brunner had earned a living by writing short stories for "pulp" magazines. Pulps were inexpensive magazines printed on cheap wood-pulp paper (hence the nickname "pulps"). They were filled with short stories, often focusing on adventure, romance, mystery, or science fiction. Fleischman credits Mr. Brunner with making him realize the most important truth about writing—"that the arts take practice."[4]

After Fleischman graduated from San Diego State, in 1949, at the age of twenty-nine, he was faced with the task of finding a job. He applied for a position at the *San Diego Daily Journal* and was hired as a copy boy, someone who takes stories from one department to another and does other errands. Not content with this, Flcischman decided to take things into his own hands. He wrote a couple of feature stories and gave them to Fred Kinne, who was the city editor (chief editor for news stories) for the paper. Mr. Kinne was impressed by the stories and moved Fleischman to the rewrite desk, where information submitted by reporters is written up and news stories are revised. About his experience there, Fleischman had this to say: "I fielded stories from the police reporter and hammered them into prose. I went out on feature stories. I reported disasters. I covered the waterfront and flower shows. I wrote obituaries."[5] He later moved on to the political beat, but without warning, the *Journal* folded, leaving Fleischman unemployed.

Paperback Writer

Following the collapse of the *Journal*, Fleischman and a coworker from the paper, Lionel Van Deerlin, started a small weekly news magazine called *Point*. The magazine made enough money to cover its expenses but not enough to pay salaries. Then, in the fall of 1950, Fawcett Publications started the Gold Medal Book imprint. The books in the imprint were original novels published in paperback. Fleischman found out that Fawcett would pay a $2,000 advance for these books. While he'd been employed by the *Journal*, Betty had given birth to a daughter, Jane. With a family to support, a $2,000 advance—good pay for the time—was attractive. Giving up his share of *Point*, Fleischman decided to take a chance and see if he could sell a book to Gold Medal.

Drawing on his experiences in Shanghai and as a newspaperman, Fleischman wrote *The Man Who Died Laughing*, the story of an American newspaperman in China. The novel was bought by Dick Carrol, an editor at Gold Medal, who changed its title to *Shanghai Flame*. The book, which was published in 1951, was a great success. The first printing of 200,000 copies sold out, and Gold Medal ordered a second printing.

Meanwhile, inspired by the success of this book, Fleischman set out to write another novel, this time an adventure story about a nightclub magician. The book was titled *Look Behind You, Lady* (1952), and it took place in

Macao, a small country in eastern Asia bordering the South China Sea.

Not long after he turned in *Look Behind You, Lady*, the Fleischmans' son, Paul, was born. (Paul Fleischman would eventually follow in his father's footsteps as a writer; he won the 1989 Newbery Medal for his book *Joyful Noise*.) Although Gold Medal turned down his next literary attempt, a spy novel, Fleischman continued to write novels.

Next, he returned to his experiences in Shanghai during the war. He decided to create a Cold War story about the attempts of Chinese villagers to escape communist China. (The Cold War was a period of political hostility between the United States and communist countries, like the U.S.S.R. and China, which took place after World War II.) In the book, the refugees attempt to cross the dangerous straits between the Chinese mainland and the island of Formosa (now Taiwan). To accomplish this, they enlist the assistance of an American merchant marine captain.

Blood Alley (as Fleischman called the book) takes its name from a street in Hongkew, an area that he explored when he was in Shanghai during the war. During World War II, many Jewish refugees fleeing from the Nazis had gone to Shanghai, and the Chinese had offered them refuge. When the Japanese invaded China, however, the Jews had been forced to move to a ghetto in Hongkew. It was here that Fleischman wandered into "a narrow, bar-lined street with the slang name Blood Alley."[6] When Fleischman was searching for a title, he remembered the street, and liking the sound of Blood Alley, used it as a name for the sea passage through which his refugees had to escape. While he was finishing the book, the Fleischmans' third child, Anne, was born.

So You Want to Be in the Movies?

The film rights to *Blood Alley* (1955) were bought by actor John Wayne's movie company, Batjac, for $5,000. According to Fleischman, "A family of five could live bountifully [well] for a year on a sum like that. I grabbed it."[7] The movie was to be directed by Bill Wellman, who had directed such famous films as *A Star Is Born* (1954). Mr. Wellman invited Fleischman to write the screenplay for the film version of his book. John Wayne and Lauren Bacall star in the movie, which was released in 1955.

Writing the screenplay for *Blood Alley* led to Fleischman writing several more movie scripts.

His new screenwriting career, which was well paid, allowed him to purchase the house in Santa Monica, California, where he still lives today. While Fleischman was at work on the movie script for his book *Yellowleg* (1960), the screenwriters went on strike and Fleischman started work on a project that would change his career forever.

4 New Wonders

Unlike other fathers, who went to work each day, Sid Fleischman did his work at home. He started writing his first children's book, *Mr. Mysterious & Company* (1962), because of an incident that took place with his daughter Jane. He recalls the story in his 1987 Newbery Medal speech:

> My daughter Jane came home waving a slip of paper that [children's book author] Leo Politi, on a visit to the children's room of the Santa Monica Public Library, had been kind enough to autograph. We crowded around to look at it, and my wife, quite innocently, remarked, "But you know,

Daddy writes books, too." It was Jane's answer that did it. "Yes," she said. "But no one reads his books."[1]

Since the screenwriters were on strike in Hollywood, Fleischman had no movie writing to do. In response to his daughter's remark, he starting writing his first children's book. Since *Yellowleg*, the movie he'd been writing prior to the screenwriters' strike, was a Western, and he'd already done a great deal of research on the Old West, he decided that the American West would be perfect setting for his book. When discussing how the book would change the direction of his career, Fleischman had this to say:

> A title flashed across my mind, and I typed it out. *Mr. Mysterious & Company*. Kind of intriguing. I improvised an opening: "It was a most remarkable sight. Even the hawks and buzzards sleeping in the blue Texas sky awoke in midair to glance down in wonder."
>
> Not bad. But what were the hawks and buzzards gazing at? Could I pry those opening sentences apart and find a story? I kept typing in order to find out.
>
> I found the story and stumbled into the wondrous world of children's books.[2]

Naturally enough, the three youngsters in *Mr. Mysterious & Company* are named after the Fleischman children: Jane, Paul, and Anne. The main protagonist is, no surprise, a magician. In *Mr. Mysterious & Company*, the main characters, the Hackett family, are wandering magicians traveling across the West to San Diego, where they plan to settle down. Their trip across the West is full of unexpected adventures and wonderful descriptions of an old-time magic show.

In the book, the main characters are outsiders—wanderers with no fixed home who are on their own. (In fact, in many of Fleischman's books, the main characters are outsiders.) Without position, power, or other people's support, they have to rely on their wits to outsmart the villains who threaten them. An example of this occurs when, at the climax of the book, they reveal the identity of the Badlands Kid, the villain of the story, by performing a magic trick, the Egyptian Box illusion. In this trick, a talking head called the Great Sphinx answers questions from the audience:

> The Egyptian Box was a foot square. It had a front door that opened on brass hinges. Pa opened the door and showed everyone that the box was empty. Then he placed it on the table.

"And now, my friends—behold!"

After a pass of his magic stick, he opened the door—slowly. The hinges creaked and shivers went up a few backs.

"The Sphinx . . ." Pa announced.

The empty box was no longer empty. A face with dark eyes looked out of the box. It was a face that looked two hundred years old![3]

The head in the box is actually the narrator, young Paul Hackett, wearing makeup that makes him look like an ancient Egyptian. In his role as question-answering head, Paul is able to tell the town's sheriff the identity of the Badlands Kid. This is, by the way, a real magic trick, in which mirrors are used to create a reflection so that a person's head, without a body, appears to be resting in a box.

In the course of selling his adult books and scripts, Fleischman acquired an agent, a person who sells a writer's work to publishers. When *Mr. Mysterious & Company* was finished, Fleischman wanted to see it in print, but he wasn't sure his agent would find a children's book interesting. Luckily, despite his concern, he went ahead and sent *Mr. Mysterious & Company* to his agent, who liked the book and sent it on to Atlantic Monthly Press, which accepted it.

Sometimes Your Career Finds You

The Hollywood writers' strike finally ended, and Sid Fleischman completed the script for *Yellowleg*. Actor Marlon Brando took an option on the screenplay. (An option is a contract that gives someone the right to produce a movie within a specified period of time.) In the end, however, Brando never made the film. Instead, Fleischman formed a film production company and made the movie under the title *The Deadly Companions*. The film is a Western set in Arizona in the 1860s. The film version of *Yellowleg* wasn't very successful. Released in 1961, the movie played in theaters for weeks (and was on television), but it didn't do well at the box office. In contrast, *Mr. Mysterious & Company* came out shortly after the film and was both a critical and a popular success. A reviewer in the *New York Times Book Review* had this to say:

> This 1884 journey of the Hackett family is light-hearted and carefree. Even their encounter with Indians and the capture of the Badlands Kid are laughing-out-loud funny.

The Hacketts' warm relationship, Jane's yearning for a friend, young Paul's high jinks, all have the ring of reality. But the author proves his genius by inventing Abracadabra Day. Once a year each child is entitled to be as wild as he likes, without fear of punishment. The day is a secret until Pa reaches for his switch. Only then does the child yell, "Abracadabra!" and all must be accepted, if not quite forgiven. A marvelous institution that may well sweep the country.[4]

Following the publication of *Mr. Mysterious & Company*, Fleischman began to receive letters from kids and invitations to speak at conferences, libraries, and schools, not just in California but around the United States. Fleischman had this to say about this period of time in his life: "Soon I was asked to speak at schools and libraries. Like [children's book author] Leo Politi, I found myself signing slips of paper in a Santa Monica library. I looked up, and there in line stood my younger daughter, Anne, age seven, with a slip of paper in her hand. She wanted my autograph, too. I knew I had arrived."[5]

Back at the Gold Rush

Authors often draw from their own experiences when creating characters, and this is also true of

Sid Fleischman. Many of the main characters he writes about are young people who go off in search of adventure. These adventurers pursue their quests—whether it's to find family or a treasure—with a sense of enthusiasm that reflects Fleischman's delight in his past of traveling around the country with the magic show.

Frequently, the young heroes of his stories are orphaned or living with a relative such as a sister or an aunt. This treatment of characters provides a convenient way of placing a young person on his or her own so that he or she must face and solve any difficulties without the interference of an adult. When Fleischman was growing up, he saw little of his father at home because he worked such long hours. Like some of his characters, Fleischman, too, came to rely on his own resources from an early age.

Fleischman draws from his professional experience working at a newspaper to create another recurring character in his books—the printer or newspaperman. For example, the father of the Hackett family, the protagonists in *Mr. Mysterious & Company,* is handy with a printing press, and the fathers of the main characters in *Humbug Mountain* (1978) and *Jim Ugly* (1992) are wandering newspapermen.

Sid Fleischman continued to take inspiration from his own experiences in *By the Great Horn Spoon!* (1963), the book he wrote after *Mr. Mysterious & Company*. In *By the Great Horn Spoon!*, he returned to his youth and the trip through the Sierra Nevada mountains that he and his friend Buddy had made as young magicians. In the course of their trip, they had visited California gold country, and it was this location that Fleischman decided to use as the setting for *By the Great Horn Spoon!* On this trip, Fleischman had tried his hand at finding gold, but without much success. However, he did strike it rich with *By the Great Horn Spoon!* The book, first published forty-one years ago, is still in print.

The phrase "By the great horn spoon!" was a fairly common exclamation of amazement in America in the late nineteenth century. It was used when referring to the constellation the Big Dipper, which was sometimes called the horn spoon. The hero of *By the Great Horn Spoon!* is an orphaned boy named Jack Flagg who lives with his Aunt Arabella in a grand old house in Boston. Aunt Arabella is running out of money and may have to sell her house as a result. Because of this, Jack sets out to make his fortune in the California gold rush. He is accompanied by his aunt's loyal and proper English butler, named Praiseworthy, who is determined to see that Jack comes to no harm.

At the beginning of the book, Jack and Praiseworthy have stowed away on a ship bound for gold country because their money has been stolen and they can't afford to pay for their passage. From that point on, the characters encounter one comic adventure after another. At first, the captain puts the pair to work shoveling coal into the steamship's boilers because he is in a race against another ship. Whoever reaches San Francisco first will win a new vessel. Thus, Jack and Praiseworthy embark on a five-month, 15,000-mile (24,140-kilometer) voyage that will test their wits as much as their strength.

In the book, Jack and Praiseworthy face difficult, dangerous, and often comic obstacles with resourcefulness and ingenuity. For example, when they find themselves desperately in need of money to pay for their transportation to the goldfields, Praiseworthy puts up a sign offering free haircuts to miners and collects the gold dust from their shorn locks until he has enough to pay for their passage. The book is not only amusing, it is also an example of the classic American dream in which anyone can become a success through hard work, regardless of background.

Writing about the gold rush involved a great deal of research. In his 1996 autobiography, *The Abracadabra Kid: A Writer's Life*, Fleischman explains how doing the research for *By the Great Horn Spoon!* led him to change his writing process:

> I wanted to cure my persistent problems with note taking on the backs of envelopes and other easily lost scraps of paper. I tinkered together a piece of research machinery.
>
> I ran out and bought a blank notebook. In order to organize my wildly ranging notes automatically, I divided the book into tabbed sections: "names," "words and expressions," "dress," "foods," "prices," "flora," "fauna," "incidents," "characters," "scenes," "ideas," and "miscellany . . ."
>
> The notebook worked . . . When I needed to dress a character, I no longer had to search through a Dumpster of random notes for a half-remembered detail. I turned to the section marked "dress," and there I'd noted that frontier San Francisco lacked skilled laundrymen and that its muddy boulevardiers sent their starched white shirts by clipper ship to China for laundering. That amazing detail, too, worked its way into the novel.[6]

Fleischman loves to use unusual and amusing-sounding names in his books. Praiseworthy's name is the result of a lucky accident. Fleischman had taken up the practice of noting interesting names in his notebook. On a drive through the San Fernando Valley in California, he'd noticed the Praisewater Mortuary. When he later recorded it at home, he mistakenly wrote the name down as "Praiseworthy." While preparing to write *By the Great Horn Spoon!*, he noticed the name in his notebook and thought that it would make a great name for a butler.

Another example of Fleischman's use of his personal experiences in his books can be seen in *The Ghost on Saturday Night* (1974). This story draws heavily on his experiences as a magician and his travels with the spook show. The book features a villain named Professor Pepper, who comes to town and promises to raise the ghost of the notorious Crookneck John. Fleischman's experience as a stage magician helped him create such a believable character. As seen in the following, Professor Pepper puts on a performance that resembles what might be seen in a spook show, and he turns out to be a superb showman.

"Now, then, I must have absolute silence!" Professor Pepper said. He clapped his hands sharply.

The curtains parted.

A pine coffin was stretched across two sawhorses. It looked old and rotted, as if it had been dug out of the ground.

"Aye, the very box holding the bones of Crookneck John," the professor declared. "The coffin is six feet long. Crookneck John was almost seven feet. Buried with his knees bent up, he was. Most uncomfortable even for a ghost."

Then Professor Pepper clapped his hands again. His assistant, the toad-faced man, appeared and blew out the two oil lamps.

Pitch darkness closed in on the hall.

For a moment, I don't think anyone took a breath.[7]

In 1999, Fleischman would return to the gold rush era for the setting of a book in which prejudice plays a major role. *Bandit's Moon* (2000) is a story about two underdogs. In the book, an orphaned girl, Annyrose, is left in the clutches of a heartless caretaker, O. O. Mary. Disguised as a boy, Annyrose sets off to find her brother Lank, who's gone to the gold diggings. However, she falls into the hands of the legendary Mexican bandit,

Joaquin Murieta. The bandit, however, is not simply the black-hearted villain she was led to believe. In the process of traveling with him, she learns of the injustices that have brought him to his present plight. A reviewer in *Publishers Weekly* praised the book, saying that Fleischman "expertly crafts a fictionalized tale that takes a clear-eyed look at bigotry and racism, while steering away from the twin pitfalls of pedantry [giving a lecture] and sermonizing [telling people how to behave]."[8] The book was yet another success for Sid Fleischman.

5 Lost Boys and Found Treasure

In the process of writing his first book, *Mr. Mysterious & Company*, Fleischman used an element that he would carry into his later children's and young adult books—humor. The books and scripts he had written for adults had all been serious in tone. However, according to Fleischman, "As a father I wanted to hear the kids laugh, and I began reaching out for funny scenes and comic villains and dialogue with flashes of humor. This novel [*Mr. Mysterious & Company*] changed me forever. It was the first sustained comic writing I had done; it fixed my style and gave me a literary voice of my own."[1]

The use of humor became one of the most notable characteristics of Fleischman's writing. Fleischman credits his third children's book, *The Ghost in the Noonday Sun* (1965), with providing the model for the funny villains he went on to create in his stories. The villain of this tale is a pirate named Captain Scratch. The hero is twelve-year-old Oliver Finch, who is at the tavern run by his Aunt Katy (who looks after him while his father is at sea) when Captain Scratch first appears. There's little doubt from his first entrance that the captain is indeed both a comic character and a villain:

> Captain Scratch seated himself at a table along the wall, and without bothering to remove his beaver hat he ate two beefsteaks and three trenchers [dishes] of chowder. He muttered a good deal to himself, ignoring the others in the room. That dark smile kept flashing across his face, and I [Oliver] heard Crick, the harpooner, mutter, "Captain Scratch, is he? From the look of him, mates, I'd as soon ship out with the Prince of Air himself!"—meaning the devil.[2]

In *The Abracadabra Kid: A Writer's Life*, Fleischman says, "My rogues [clever villains] wear fright wigs, but they also wear putty noses and slap shoes."[3] Indeed, Captain Scratch was to be followed by a long line of dastardly yet comic villains, such as Mrs. Daggatt, the greedy, bombastic orphanage keeper of *Jingo Django* (1971); Professor Pepper, the ghost raiser and robber in *The Ghost on Saturday Night* (1974); and the conniving Judge Wigglesworth in *The Midnight Horse* (1990).

The Ghost in the Noonday Sun is based on an old superstition that a child born exactly at midnight will be able to see ghosts. In the book, the evil pirates, led by Captain Scratch, have buried treasure on an island but can't remember how to get there. The pirate captain is convinced that the ghost of the previous captain of the pirate ship (who died on the island) guards the treasure. He believes that if they could follow the captain's ghost, the ghost would lead them to the treasure.

Unfortunately, in order to follow the ghost, they'd have to be able to see it, so Captain Scratch kidnaps Oliver to help him. Because Oliver was born at the stroke of midnight, the captain hopes that Oliver will be able to see the ghost and thus lead them to the treasure. What happens next is a lively pirate adventure.

Despite getting his just reward at the end of the book, this is not the last that is heard of Captain

Scratch. He makes a brief return appearance in *The 13th Floor: A Ghost Story* (1995). In 1974, a comedic film version of *The Ghost in the Noonday Sun* was made in which Peter Sellers played Captain Scratch, but it never appeared in theaters, although it was released on video.

Fleischman says, "I feel secure when I have a good comic villain who is also threatening. A cunning but lovable con man gives me situations I can work with, by using sleight-of-mind [clever tricks]. Sometimes I have to spend a long time thrashing a way out of a situation."[4]

When crafting his books, Fleischman works hard at making characters and their words sound funny. As he says, "Writing humor takes a knack and experience . . . You learn to balance a sentence, to end it with the right choice of words that makes it funny."[5]

Tall Tales and Words of Ice

Fleischman's interest in writing humorous stories led him to become a writer of tall tales—a type of traditional American folk story. Folk stories are tales that are made up and told by ordinary people rather than professional writers. These stories feature exaggerated and unlikely events and characters, and they are often very funny. The legend of Paul Bunyan, for example, is an American tall tale.

Many critics are impressed by Fleischman's ability to write tall tales. For instance, a review in *Children's Literature in the Elementary School*, noted that, "[Sid Fleischman is] becoming a master at creating modern tall tales. *Chancy and the Grand Rascal* is the story of a young orphan who sets out to find his brothers and sisters but first meets his uncle, the Grand Rascal, who can out-talk, out-laugh, and out-fox any man on the river."[6]

Chancy and the Grand Rascal (1966) was significant for Fleischman because it was the first time he wrote a book that was primarily a tall tale. Chancy, a teenage orphan, is the hero of the book, which is set just after the American Civil War. After the death of his parents, he and his brothers and sisters were sent to live with people in different places around the Midwest. At the start of the book, Chancy sets out to find his brothers and sisters. Before long, however, he runs into his uncle, the Grand Rascal, who is on the same quest. At their first meeting, the Grand Rascal has this to say:

> Why, Chancy, I'm a coming-and-going man, that's who I am! I can shoe a runaway horse and out-calculate a pack of foxes. I'm half fox myself, and the other half prairie buffalo! I'm a wayfaring printer, mule skinner, soldier, tinkerer, barn painter, and everything in between. I've been clear to California and I once pulled a wagon with my teeth. If that don't suit you, why, I can out-laugh, out-exaggerate, and out-rascal any man this side of the Big Muddy, and twice as many on the other![7]

This passage illustrates some typical characteristics of tall tales. The characters, like the Grand Rascal, are larger than life. The language has a rhythm typical of country speech, and a lot of colorful phrases and country slang are used—for example, referring to the Missouri River as "the Big Muddy." Exaggeration is another feature of tall tales. Indeed, it's unlikely that the Grand Rascal ever really pulled a wagon with his teeth, but as he says, he can out-exaggerate anyone.

In a rave review of *Chancy and the Grand Rascal*, author Jane Yolen says:

> For all readers who adore braggadocio [bragging] and consider Paul Bunyan and Pecos Bill the apogee [height] of American humor, *Chancy and the Grand Rascal* is a

godsend [blessing]. A perfect blend of one part quest story and two parts tall tale, it is one of the finest and funniest juvenile books to be written in a long while.[8]

Sid Fleischman's most famous tall tales, however, are the series of books he wrote from 1966 to 1982 about a Midwestern farmer named McBroom. McBroom started out as a minor character in *Chancy and the Grand Rascal*. When Fleischman needed to find some type of contest to show off the Grand Rascal's wit, he had him face off against the captain of a river raft in a contest to see who could tell the most outrageous lie. For the contest, Fleischman came up with "a lie about a farmer on a one-acre farm with earth so rich he could plant and harvest three crops a day."[9] Although this was the character's only appearance in print, Fleischman was sufficiently amused by the idea of the whimsical tall tale farmer that he decided to give him a book of his own.

Fleischman gave his new character a name, a family, and an enemy named Heck Jones, "whose own land was so pickax-hard he had to plant seeds with a shotgun."[10] When he was done typing, he had the first of the McBroom books, *McBroom Tells the Truth*. An example of one of these clever tales is *McBroom's Ghost*, in which McBroom and his family are plagued by mysterious voices talking when there is no one around. When, despite their efforts to uncover the source of the words, no explanation can be found, the characters are convinced they are being harassed by ghosts. The voices, however, simply turn out to be words that were frozen during winter that are now being heard as they thaw out in the spring.

This story points at one of the key features of tall tales: the events may be exaggerated or even absurd, but whatever happens, no matter how silly, must follow logically from the details of the world in which the characters live.

The Bloodhound Gang

In the early 1980s, Fleischman wrote a number of scripts for a children's television show in which a group of teenage detectives used logic and science to solve mysteries. He later turned these stories into a series of mystery books featuring the Bloodhound Gang. Fleischman would go on to write five Bloodhound Gang books: *The Bloodhound Gang in the Case of the Cackling Ghost* (1981), *The Bloodhound Gang in the Case of the Flying Clock* (1981), *The*

Bloodhound Gang in the Case of the Secret Message (1981), *The Bloodhound Gang in the Case of Princess Tomorrow* (1981), and *The Bloodhound Gang in the Case of the 264 Pound Burglar* (1982).

Sid Fleischman was, however, soon to return to history for his inspiration, with surprising results.

6 Spoiled Brats and Noble Waifs

In his Newbery Medal speech, Fleischman recounted:

> I stumbled across the catapulting idea for *The Whipping Boy* while researching historical materials for another project. I checked the dictionary [for "whipping boy"]. "A boy," it confirmed, "educated with a prince and punished in his stead." My literary pulse began to pound. The common phrase as historical fact. What an outrageous practice, I thought. Here was a story I wanted to write, and with two main characters already provided, I'd make quick work of it. It was as if history had set a trap in its pages, waiting for me to step into it.[1]

As it turned out, *The Whipping Boy* took longer to write than he anticipated, and Fleischman worked on it on and off for several years before he was finally satisfied with the story. But the wait was worth it. *The Whipping Boy* was finally published in 1986, and the following year, it won the Newbery Medal, awarded by the American Library Association's Library Service to Children for the most distinguished American children's book.

The Whipping Boy is the story of two boys. The first is a spoiled young prince, Horace, appropriately called Prince Brat by those who have to put up with his obnoxious ways. The other is a resourceful young whipping boy, Jemmy, who must take whatever punishment is due the prince, since it is forbidden to lay hands on the prince himself. When the prince is bad, which is often, it's Jemmy who is punished.

As far as Jemmy (the son of a rat catcher) is concerned, the quality of the food, clothes, and accommodations he receives at the palace doesn't make up for what he has to put up with. He longs to return to his own life on the streets. When the prince runs away from home, however, it's up to the whipping boy to see that he comes to no harm, not an easy task once the pair fall into the hands of Hold-Your-Nose Billy. Hold-Your-Nose Billy is one of Sid Fleischman's most memorable villains. He's an outlaw with a taste for garlic, which is the reason for his name. This resulted in a ballad being written about him:

> Hold-Your-Nose Billy, a wild man is he.
>
> Hang him from a gallows tree.
>
> Here he comes, there he goes:
>
> Don't forget to hold your nose.[2]

This wasn't the end of the line for *The Whipping Boy*. The book was made into a movie, too. However, the author credit for the movie is given as Max Brindle rather than Sid Fleischman. Fleischman really did write the screenplay, but when the producers made a change in the story that he thought made no sense, he decided to use a pseudonym instead of his real name. Max Brindle is a character he made up as the hero of his very first detective novel.

An important feature of Sid Fleischman's writing is the use of a humorous situation to make a point about a serious issue. As Fleischman said in an article, "It's only the surface that's humorous. Usually, I take a frightening situation and deal with it in comic terms."[3] *The Whipping Boy* is a good example of this. Although Prince Brat and Jemmy's adventures with Hold-Your-Nose Billy are amusing, Fleischman uses *The Whipping Boy* to make a point about how damaging quick assumptions about people can be. In the book, both boys see each other through the roles they have in society. However, through their experiences, they learn to view each other as individuals who have more in common than they thought. A reviewer in the *New York Times Book Review* had this to say:

> As Sid Fleischman's story unfolds this updated pauper and his prince are kidnapped and, in trying to escape, swap identities. The consequences of the trade irrevocably transform each boy. By the end both have inklings about how the other got to be the way he is, and both have seen below the facile [easy] adjectives that describe the other to the feelings and experiences that produced them . . . "The Whipping Boy" offers something special. Jemmy learns to sympathize with the Prince's isolation, boredom and constricted life. He learns to admire his courage in facing dangers . . . And, in his journey with Horace, he

tastes a friendship based on more than struggle and deprivation [lack].

Horace, on the other hand, arrives at an altered sense of his own life after living it without protective batting for a while. Once he experiences his own strength, he can admire Jemmy's without seeing it as a taunt. When he discovers that the people in his kingdom refer to him as Prince Brat and fear the day when he will become king he has traveled far enough on his own to admit both the pain and the justice of the appellation [name]. He is able to do so because he has grown strong enough to change.[4]

And children's book writer Jane Yolen raved, "Fleischman's wit and style are deceptive. His flagrant humor disguises the fact that he is a careful craftsman who chooses each scene with infinite care and sets it down with a straight face."[5]

7 The Art of Writing

Sid Fleischman works at a large cluttered table covered with the tools of his trade in "an old-fashioned, two-story house full of creaks and character"[1] in Santa Monica, California, overlooking the ocean. He is a disciplined writer, who settles down to write regularly in the morning, generally working an hour or two, taking a break for breakfast, and then returning to work some more. He is the type of writer who doesn't plot out the entire story in advance but works it out as he goes along.

It generally takes Fleischman from three months to a year to write a book and sometimes "much longer if [I] can't figure out how to get his characters out of the jams [I have] put them in."[2]

Some writers prefer to write the first draft of a book quickly and then go back and revise the story as necessary. Fleischman, however, prefers to polish each page as he writes it, going over one word at at time on each page until he's satisfied. In *The Abracadabra Kid: A Writer's Life*, he says, "I write the first page once, twice, ten or twenty times before I get everything as right as I can. Only then do I move on to the second page, and the third. I used to trash reams of paper over minor changes in the text. The computer has made the whole process easier, less wasteful, and less exhausting."[3]

Fleischman does a lot of research for his books. He especially likes to read the diaries and journals of people who lived a long time ago. In them he finds many interesting phrases and superstitions, which sometimes find their way into his books. Fleischman doesn't like to visit the actual location he's using in the story he's writing, however. He says the following: "My creative juices rise out of research almost entirely—that's where my imagination rummages around and is freed. The past is very much like fantasy since I can't really see or touch it except by leaps of imagination."[4] After he completes his research, he lets his imagination take over and creates his own version of the past, with its colorful language, comic villains, and exciting adventures.

Fleischman uses a skill he calls "sleight of mind" in plotting his stories. He credits his past experience as a magician with developing his delight in surprise and mystery and his skill at clever misdirection. This "sleight of mind" is an ability to cleverly misdirect or fool the villains who threaten his main characters. For instance, when a villain, Ed Blackberry, threatens Pa Hackett in *Mr. Mysterious & Company*, Pa pretends to be color-blind. He points to a gold nugget and says it's green, like the rocks he saw in the distance. This causes Ed Blackberry to rush off to seek what he's sure is gold.

Fleischman is not concerned about the fact that he doesn't plot out his books in advance. As he says, "It doesn't worry me that I don't know where I'm going. But I know I'll know it when I get there. Writing for me, like life itself, is a daily improvisation. Who knows what surprises lurk in the typewriter!"[5] The advantage of Fleischman's approach to writing is that it keeps his interest while he's working on a story. He is excited about getting back to his writing each morning because he wants to find out what happens next, rather than dreading having to write through a difficult part of the story as some writers do.

So You Want to Be a Writer

In *The Abracadabra Kid: A Writer's Life*, Fleischman says,

> Writing a novel is a one-person job. You design the sets; you put lamps in the rooms and pictures on the walls; you dress the actors and describe their fleeting expressions. You are the ringmaster and all the acts, and you sweep up at night.[6]

He does, however, offer extremely useful suggestions for aspiring writers, including:

> 1. It's best that the hero or heroine end up solving the major problem in a story—and not a secondary character.

> 2. The experiences that the main character has in a story should ultimately change him or her.

3. Dramatize important scenes and describe the minor ones, instead of the other way around.

4. When writing a story, break it down into scenes—similar to what you see when watching a movie. This creates a more dramatic effect.

5. To build a sense of excitement and suspense in a story, tease readers by giving them small pieces of information.

After forty years of writing, Sid Fleischman still retains his enthusiasm for the profession that he discovered by accident:

> While my books rarely draw upon direct personal experience, I catch ghostly glimpses of my presence on almost every page. The stories inevitably reveal my interests and enthusiasms—my taste for the comic in life, my love of adventure, the seductions [lure] (for me) of the 19th-century American frontier, and my enchantment with the folk speech of that period. Language is a wondrous toy and I have great literary fun with it.[7]

New Horizons

Sid Fleischman's most recent book, *Disappearing Act* (2003)—about a brother and sister who flee to the zany and colorful boardwalk in Venice,

California, to escape a stalker—was published just as this book went to press. His book prior to *Disappearing Act* was *Bo & Mzzz Mad*, published in 2001, when Fleischman was eighty-one. The story is something of a change for him. Although it is set in the American West, it takes place in the present.

The book is about two feuding families, the Gamages and the Martinkas, each of whom assumes the other has stolen a map to a gold mine from one of their ancestors. When Bo Gamage is orphaned, he takes a bus to the California desert to avoid being sent to a foster home. There he meets Aunt Juna and Charles Martinka, an ex-cowboy star, who are hunting for the lost Pegleg Smith gold mine. He also meets Madeleine Martinka, a girl about his own age, and it's hate at first sight. Madeleine, who's nicknamed Mzzz Mad, and Bo are forced to join forces, however, when the family is threatened by robbers on the run.

A review in *Booklist* shows that Sid Fleischman is as equally adept at handling contemporary subject matter as he is with historical fiction:

> A less talented writer might not have been able to bring the novel's several story lines together. But Fleischman does a first-rate job, using some clever twists and snappy repartee

[a quick and witty reply]. Interchanges between Bo and Mzzz Mad are great fun, and the characters—from lonely, angry Bo to the surprising ruthless young thieves—are a sturdy bunch. Even the secret of the map is unraveled with panache [dash or flamboyance].[8]

There is something special about being a writer of books for young people, according to Fleischman. He says, "The books we enjoy as children stay with us forever—they have a special impact. Paragraph after paragraph and page after page, the author must deliver his or her best work."[9]

Interview with Sid Fleischman

Jeri Freedman: Which of your books is your favorite and why?

Sid Fleischman: Hard to say. *Mr. Mysterious & Company* because I put my three kids into it. *The Whipping Boy* because it won the Newbery. *By the Great Horn Spoon!* because it's the most accomplished—and the sunniest.

Jeri Freedman: What is your routine when writing a book?

Sid Fleischman: I'm at my desk before breakfast, right out of bed. Write for an hour or two, then break for a shower and something to eat. Return to the novel in progress (as it usually is) on and off throughout the day and often into the night. I compose directly on the computer, rewriting as I go along.

Jeri Freedman: Who were some of your earliest inspirations and favorite books? What books did you read as a child?

Sid Fleischman: The usual senior citizens of lit [literature]—Robin Hood, Huck Finn, Tom Sawyer. I missed the usual junk reading of childhood (Hardy Boys, etc.), as I was too busy reading up on how to become a magician.

Jeri Freedman: Your characters often have unusual names. How do you decide on the names of your characters?

Sid Fleischman: I keep name lists and jot down anything interesting that comes along. Then, when I need to name a character, I run through my collection until one jumps out at me. That's where I found the name for a tall tale–telling farmer—McBroom. And even Hold-Your-Nose-Billy in *The Whipping Boy* was actually someone's nickname way back.

Jeri Freedman: Are you currently working on a book? If so, what is it about and where did this story come from?

Interview with Sid Fleischman

Sid Fleischman: Just finished one, *Disappearing Act*, published by Greenwillow/HarperCollins. The story deals with street performers. The story came out of thin air—well, almost. I saw a mannequin act (as those people posing as statues, without blinking their eyes, are called) in Honolulu [Hawaii], and that set me off on the novel, though I changed the background to Venice, California, close to where I live in Santa Monica. More convenient to research.

Jeri Freedman: What do you enjoy most about writing? What do you dislike?

Sid Fleischman: I used to hate writing when I didn't know what I was doing. Once I caught on I began to enjoy the daily labors, and still do. I find it exciting to launch a few characters on an adventure of some sort, never knowing myself how it will all turn out. Because I keep myself (and, I hope, the reader) guessing. I'm not one of those writers who sharpen a gross of pencils before being able to settle down to work. I'm anxious to start in order to find out what's going to happen next in my story.

Jeri Freedman: You have written material such as screenplays for adults as well as young adult books. What are the similarities and differences between writing for adults and writing for young people?

Sid Fleischman: I hardly notice the difference since the basic principles of story writing are the same for each. The screenplay form on the page is quite different with scene numbers, etc., and I am always aware that I am writing visually for the camera. When writing for young people, I am writing just as visually, but I am aware of the young audience I hope will be turning the pages. Naturally, there is some subject matter for adults that I don't care to deal with for kids—bloody murder, for example.

Timeline

1920 Sid Fleischman is born on March 16.
1922 Fleischman moves to San Diego, California.
1934 Fleischman joins the Magicians Club of San Diego.
1936 Fleischman and Buddy Ryan take their See'n Is Believ'n magic show on a road trip through the Sierra Nevada mountains.
1939 Fleischman's first book, *Between Cocktails*, is published.
1941 Fleischman is called up for active duty in the navy as the United States enters World War II.
1942 Fleischman marries Betty Taylor.

1948 Fleischman's first novel, *The Straw Donkey Case*, is published by Phoenix Press.
1949 Fleischman graduates from San Diego State College and goes to work for the *San Diego Daily Journal*.
1955 The film version of Fleischman's book *Blood Alley* is released.
1958 The film version of Fleischman's book *Lafayette Escadrille* is released.
1961 The film version of Fleischman's book *Yellowleg* is released.
1962 Fleischman's first children's book, *Mr. Mysterious & Company*, is published.
1963 *By the Great Horn Spoon!* is published and wins the Spur Award from the Western Writers of America.
1965 *The Ghost in the Noonday Sun* is published.
1966 *Chancy and the Grand Rascal* and *McBroom Tells the Truth* are published.
1967 *McBroom and the Big Wind* is published, and the film *Bullwhip Griffin*, based on Fleischman's book *By the Great Horn Spoon!*, is released.
1970 *Longbeard the Wizard* and *McBroom's Ear* are published.
1971 *Jingo Django, McBroom's Ghost,* and *McBroom's Zoo* are published.

Timeline

1972 *The Wooden Cat Man* is published.
1973 *McBroom the Rainmaker* is published.
1974 *The Ghost on Saturday Night* is published.
1975 *McBroom Tells a Lie* and *Mr. Mysterious's Book of Magic* are published.
1977 *Me and the Man on the Moon-Eyed Horse* is published.
1978 *Humbug Mountain, Jim Bridger's Alarm Clock,* and *McBroom and the Beanstalk* are published.
1979 Fleischman wins the Horn Book Award for *Humbug Mountain.The Hey Hey Man* is published.
1980 *McBroom and the Great Race* is published.
1981 *The Bloodhound Gang in the Case of the Cackling Ghost, The Bloodhound Gang in the Case of the Flying Clock, Random, The Bloodhound Gang in the Case of the Secret Message,* and *The Bloodhound Gang in the Case of Princess Tomorrow* are published.
1982 *The Bloodhound Gang in the Case of the 264 Pound Burglar, McBroom's Almanac,* and *McBroom's Wonderful One-Acre Farm* are published.
1986 *The Whipping Boy* is published.
1987 Fleischman wins the Newbery Medal for *The Whipping Boy*.
1988 *The Scarebird* is published.
1990 *The Midnight Horse* is published.

1992 *Here Comes McBroom!* and *Jim Ugly* are published.
1995 *The 13th Floor: A Ghost Story* is published.
1996 *The Abracadabra Kid: A Writer's Life* is published.
1998 *Bandit's Moon* is published.
1999 *The Ghost in the Noonday Sun* is published.
2000 *A Carnival of Animals* is published.
2001 *Bo and Mzzz Mad* is published.
2003 *Disappearing Act* is published.

Selected Reviews from *School Library Journal*

The Abracadabra Kid: A Writer's Life
September 1996

Gr 5 Up—In a chatty style, this Newbery-award winning author of over thirty children's books converses about his "three lives." As a child, Fleischman was introduced to the world of magic, and was so enthralled by it that he read every book about it that the San Diego Public Library had to offer. Later, he traveled the country, performing in town halls, vaudeville theaters, and clubs. When he couldn't make big paychecks appear, he wrote a book of magic tricks, *Between Cocktails*, which has been in print for fifty years. Then he went back to school to study writing and again utilized the public library's resources. After military service he worked as a screenwriter. Had the Hollywood screen writers not gone on strike, children's literature may have been deprived of a great writer. During the strike he wrote *Mr. Mysterious & Company* (Little, 1962) and was amazed by the enthusiastic response it got from young readers. Casual in tone, Fleischman's words sparkle with sly humor and clever phrasing: "In those days, I was no literary diamond in the rough—I wasn't even a zircon." Each chapter is prefaced by choice excerpts from his fan mail. A professional magician to the end, Fleischman does not give away his signature magic tricks; nor does he leave his audience empty-handed. Instead, he presents youngsters with his favorite writing tips. This book is the next best thing to having the author visit your school or library and will be a boon to all those assigned to read an autobiography. —Marilyn Payne Phillips, University City Public Library, Missouri

Bo & Mzzz Mad
2001

Gr 4–7—Fleischman's many fans won't be disappointed by this fast-paced tale. The story is set in a tiny Western town that really isn't a town at all—it's just the remnants of a Western movie set, stuck in the California desert. Recently orphaned Bo Gamage decides to visit his only remaining relatives, despite a longstanding family feud between the Gamages and Martinkas. The twelve-year-old discovers that Queen of Sheba's only residents are his great-uncle Charlie Martinka, a washed-up, cantankerous cowboy actor; Aunt Juna; and cousin Madeleine, a thirteen-year-old who calls herself "Mzzz Mad." The feud centers on an alleged gold mine in the nearby hills, which both sides of the family claim but no one can find. It's not long before Bo realizes that he would like to go back to the city life he's used to and escape the bad blood, but the realities of the harsh desert keep him from walking away. Then, a couple of modern-day bandits arrive on the scene and hold the family hostage. The resulting troubles draw the relatives together and the mystery surrounding the contentious gold mine is solved. The narrative speeds along with enough plot twists to keep readers flipping pages. Character development suffers a little, the conflict between the title characters is a bit superficial, and the resolution is not very satisfying. Charlie Martinka, however, is colorful and charming, still clanking around in his spurs and cowboy delusions. The combination of his character and Fleischman's storytelling prowess results in a fun, quick read. —Steve Clancy, Colonial Village Elementary School, Niagara Falls, New York

The Midnight Horse
Illustrated by Peter Sis
September 1990

It's "raining bullfrogs" when readers first meet the skinny and bareheaded orphan boy Touch with his hair "as curly as wood shavings." Touch is en route—by horse-drawn coach—to Cricklewood, New Hampshire, where he will meet his great-uncle and only surviving relative, Judge Henry Wigglesforth. The boy's traveling companions are an honest blacksmith, a mysterious thief, and a shadowy figure on the coach's roof. "Merciful powers!" the blacksmith exclaims, "It's The Great Chaffalo!" It seems that since the magician became a ghost, he has developed the disconcerting habit of turning up in odd and unexpected places. How he becomes Touch's ally against the conniving Judge Wigglesforth readers will delight in discovering for themselves. The process is pure pleasure. Fleischman—who has always had a fondness for magicians—has himself become a master magician with words, producing dazzling and seemingly effortless rhetorical effects from his writer's sleeve. How he does it is his secret, but it surely has something to do with inspired plotting, masterful timing, and a wonderful ear for comic language, lively dialogue, and the best similes and metaphors this side of Leon Garfield. The illustrations by the talented Sis perfectly capture the spirit of the text while complementing its substance. The book is part ghost story, part tall tale, part picaresque, and totally enjoyable, for it is that old enchanter Sid Fleischman at his magical best. —Michael Cart, Beverly Hills Public Library, Beverly Hills, California

Jim Ugly
Illustrated by Jos. A. Smith
April 1992

Gr 4–8—With a little silent-movie piano accompaniment, this rollicking parody of Western melodrama would effortlessly unfold across any stage. It is 1894, and Jake Bannock's actor father, Sam, has just been buried. The twelve-year-old boy is seemingly left an orphan with no inheritance except for an unnamed, one-man dog, "part elkhound, part something else, and a large helping of short-eared timber wolf." Jake calls him Jim Ugly. Mystery arises immediately. Where are the diamonds his dad is accused of stealing? Was that really Dad buried there in the Nevada Desert at Blowfly? Jake sets out in search of the answers, aided by Jim Ugly's keen nose. The two travel by baggage car from one town to another, trying to avoid a bounty-hunting, former cavalry sergeant who villainously skulks around the story's corners. Jake tells his own adventurous story—how he meets Wilhelmina Marlybone-Jenkins, an actress who was Sam's sweetheart; how he plays the apple-balancing role of William Tell's son with a traveling theatrical troupe; and how his search pays off when he sees his father—alive and well—on a San Francisco trolley. The climax and resolution make for a wonderfully improbable, mesquite flavored, farce. Jake's voice is simple and direct, made vivid by Fleischman's command of simile and metaphor. —Katharine Bruner, Brown Middle School, Harrison, Tennessee

List of Selected Works

The Abracadabra Kid: A Writer's Life. New York: Greenwillow Books, 1996.
Bandit's Moon. Illustrated by Jos. A. Smith. New York: Greenwillow Books, 1998.
The Bloodhound Gang in the Case of the Cackling Ghost. Illustrated by Anthony Rao. New York: Random House, 1981.
The Bloodhound Gang in the Case of the Flying Clock. Illustrated by William Harmuth. New York: Random House, 1981.
The Bloodhound Gang in the Case of Princess Tomorrow. Illustrated by Bill Morrison. New York: Random House, 1981.
The Bloodhound Gang in the Case of the Secret Message. New York: Random House, 1981.

The Bloodhound Gang in the Case of the 264 Pound Burglar. Illustrated by Bill Morrison. New York: Random House, 1982.

Bo & Mzzz Mad. New York: Greenwillow Books, 2001.

By the Great Horn Spoon! Illustrated by Eric von Schmidt. New York: Atlantic Monthly Press, 1963.

A Carnival of Animals. Illustrated by Marilyn Hafner. New York: Greenwillow Books, 2000.

Chancy and the Grand Rascal. Illustrated by Eric von Schmidt. New York: Atlantic Monthly Press, 1966.

Disappearing Act. New York: HarperCollins, 2003.

The Ghost in the Noonday Sun. Illustrated by Warren Chappell. New York: Little, Brown, and Company, 1965.

The Ghost on Saturday Night. Illustrated by Eric von Schmidt. New York: Atlantic Monthly Press, 1974.

Here Comes McBroom! New York: Greenwillow Books, 1992.

The Hey Hey Man. New York: Atlantic Monthly Press, 1979.

Humbug Mountain. Illustrated by Eric von Schmidt. New York: Atlantic Monthly Press, 1978.

Jim Bridger's Alarm Clock. Illustrated by Eric von Schmidt. New York: Dutton, 1978.

List of Selected Works

Jim Ugly. Illustrated by Jos. A. Smith. New York: Greenwillow Books, 1992.

Jingo Django. Illustrated by Eric von Schmidt. New York: Atlantic Monthly Press, 1971.

Longbeard the Wizard. Illustrated by Charles Bragg. New York: Atlantic Monthly Press, 1970.

McBroom and the Big Wind. Illustrated by Kurt Werth. New York: Norton, 1967.

McBroom and the Great Race. New York: Atlantic Monthly Press, 1980.

McBroom's Almanac. Illustrated by Walter Lorraine. New York: Atlantic Monthly Press, 1982.

McBroom's Ear. Illustrated by Kurt Werth. New York: Norton, 1970.

McBroom's Ghost. Illustrated by Robert Frankenberg. New York: Atlantic Monthly Press, 1971.

McBroom's Wonderful One-Acre Farm. Illustrated by Marilyn Hafner. New York: HarperCollins, 1982.

McBroom's Zoo. Illustrated by Kurt Werth. New York: Grosset, 1971.

McBroom Tells a Lie. Illustrated by Walter Lorraine. New York: Little, Brown, 1975.

McBroom Tells the Truth. New York: Norton, 1966.

McBroom the Rainmaker. Illustrated by Walter Lorraine. New York: Grosset, 1973.

Me and the Man on the Moon-Eyed Horse. Illustrated by Eric von Schmidt. New York: Little, Brown, 1977.

The Midnight Horse. Illustrated by Peter Sis. New York: Greenwillow Books, 1990.

Mr. Mysterious & Company. Illustrated by Eric von Schmidt. New York: Atlantic Monthly Press, 1962.

Mr. Mysterious's Secrets of Magic. New York: Atlantic Monthly Press, 1975.

The Scarebird. Illustrated by Peter Sis. New York: Greenwillow Books, 1988.

The 13th Floor: A Ghost Story. Illustrated by Peter Sis. New York: Greenwillow Books, 1995.

The Whipping Boy. Illustrated by Peter Sis. New York: Greenwillow Books, 1986.

The Wooden Cat Man. Illustrated by Peter Yang. New York: Atlantic Monthly Press, 1972.

List of Selected Awards

Southern California Children's Books Association Golden Dolphin Award (2002) for lifetime achievement and contributions in the field of literature for children and young adults.

***The Abracadabra Kid: A Writer's Life* (1996)**
American Library Association Notable Book (1997)

***Bandit's Moon* (1998)**
American Library Association Notable Book (1999)
South Carolina Junior Book Awards Nominee (2001–2002)

By the Great Horn Spoon! **(1963)**
Junior Book Award (1964)
Southern California Council on Literature for Children and Young People Award (1964)
Western Writers of America Spur Award (1964)

The Ghost on Saturday Night **(1974)**
Mark Twain Award, presented by the Missouri Association of School Librarians (1977)
Young Hoosier Award, given by the Association for Indiana Media Educators (1979)

Humbug Mountain **(1978)**
The *Boston Globe/Horn Book* Award (1979)
National Book Award Finalist (1979)
School Library Journal Best of the Best Books 1966–1978

Jim Ugly **(1992)**
Parent's Choice Award (1992)

Jingo Django **(1971)**
American Library Association Notable Book (1971)

McBroom Tells the Truth **(1966)**
Lewis B. Carroll Shelf Award (1966)

List of Selected Awards

***McBroom the Rainmaker* (1973)**
Society of Children's Book Writers Honor Book, Golden Kite Award (1974)

***The Midnight Horse* (1990)**
Parent's Choice Award (1990)

***Mr. Mysterious & Company* (1962)**
The *Boston Globe/Horn Book* Award (1966)

***The Scarebird* (1988)**
The International Reading Association's Paul A. Witty Award (1988)

***The Whipping Boy* (1986)**
Newbery Medal (1987)

Glossary

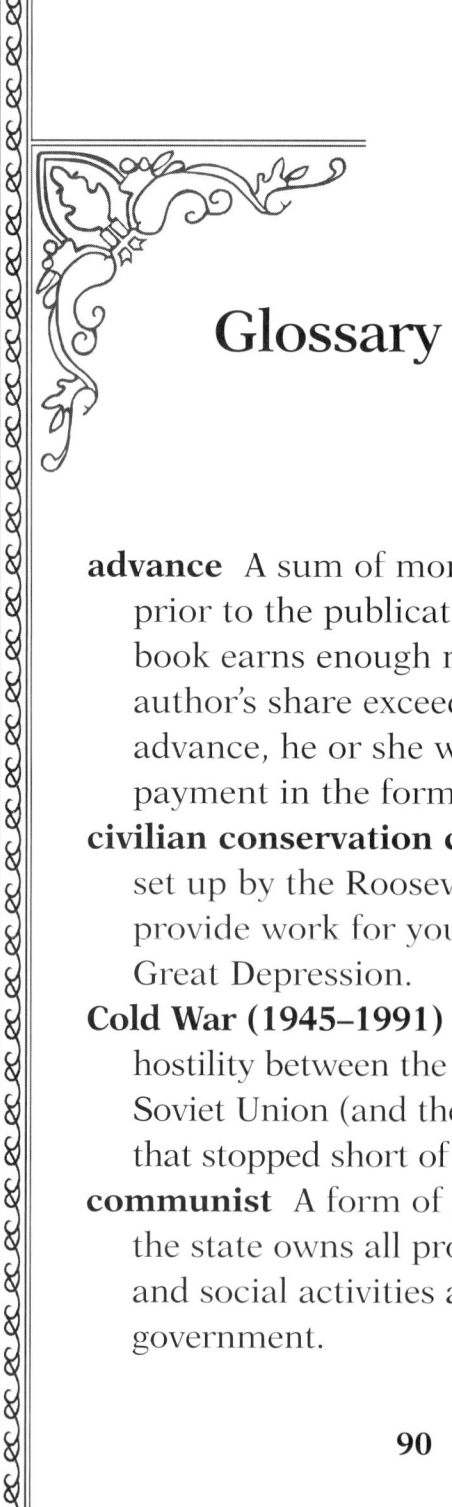

advance A sum of money paid to an author prior to the publication of a work; if a book earns enough money so that the author's share exceeds the amount of the advance, he or she will receive additional payment in the form of royalties.

civilian conservation camps Work camps set up by the Roosevelt administration to provide work for young men during the Great Depression.

Cold War (1945–1991) A period of political hostility between the United States and the Soviet Union (and their respective allies) that stopped short of military action.

communist A form of government in which the state owns all property, and economic and social activities are controlled by the government.

Glossary

convoy A group of ships traveling together.

copy boy Someone at a newspaper who takes stories from one place to another and does errands.

destroyer escort An armed naval vessel designed to protect less heavily armed ships.

dialect An accent and turn of phrase that is unique to a specific geographic area.

Great Depression The period from October 1929 to the late 1930s, when the United States economy was in poor shape and millions of people were out of work.

handbill A piece of paper with information advertising an event that is handed out or posted.

merchant marine Ships engaged in commerce, as opposed to military ships.

option The right to use written or other material to produce a movie or other type of performance within an agreed-upon period of time.

phosphorescent Glowing in the dark. This effect is often achieved by painting objects with a type of paint that absorbs light and then glows in the dark when the lights are turned off.

pseudonym A made-up name an author uses rather than his or her real name.

pulps Fiction magazines containing short stories by various writers, printed on cheap wood-pulp paper.

royalties A percentage of the selling price of a book that an author receives.

screenplay The script from which a movie is made.

serial A type of television or radio show in which the story is told in a series of weekly episodes.

sleight of hand Magic tricks that rely on a magician's ability to move and hide objects with his or her hands (such as tricks with coins and cards).

spook show A show consisting of spooky effects and magic tricks, usually performed in a movie theater after the regular program.

strait A narrow passage of water between two areas of land; it connects two larger bodies of water.

subsidize To provide money to a person for support while that person engages in an activity such as attending college.

superstition An irrational belief in the properties of an object or the significance of an act or occurrence.

Glossary

sweatshop Factories where people labor in harsh working conditions.

vaudeville A form of live variety show popular in the nineteenth and early twentieth centuries.

For More Information

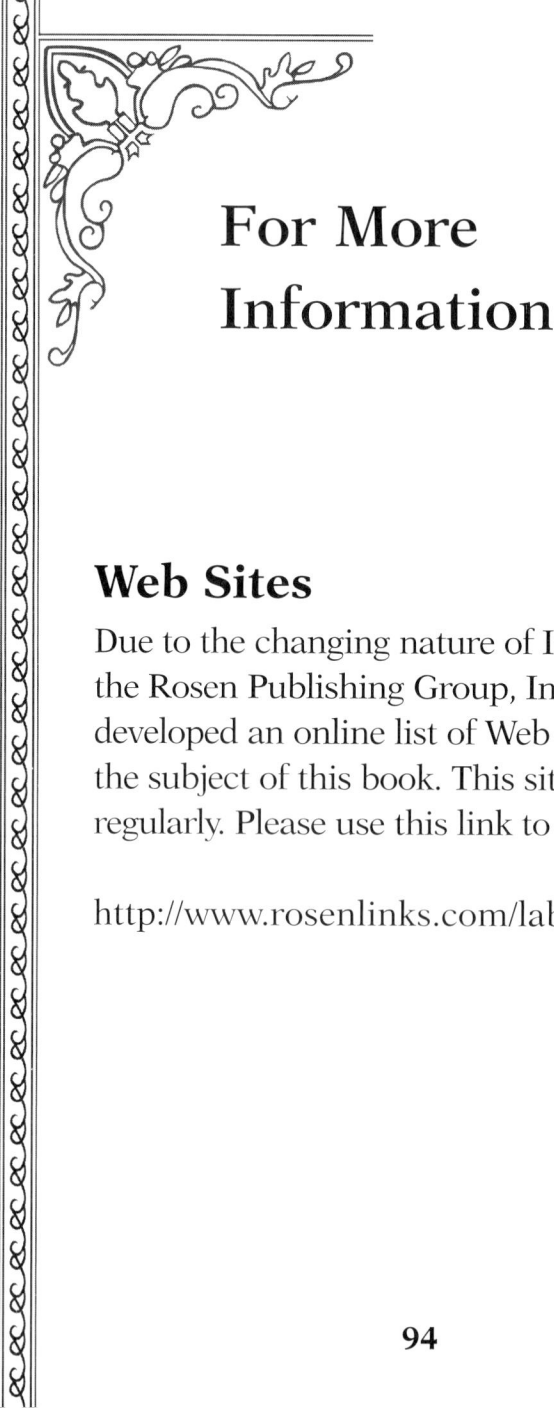

Web Sites

Due to the changing nature of Internet links, the Rosen Publishing Group, Inc., has developed an online list of Web sites related to the subject of this book. This site is updated regularly. Please use this link to access the list:

http://www.rosenlinks.com/lab/sfle

For Further Reading

Encyclopedia of Frontier and Western Fiction. New York: McGraw-Hill, 1983.

Fleischman, Sid. "Newbery Medal Acceptance." *The Horn Book Magazine*, July–August 1987.

Fleischman, Paul. "Sid Fleischman." *The Horn Book Magazine*, July–August 1987.

Fleischman, Sid. *The Abracadabra Kid: A Writer's Life*. New York: Greenwillow Books, 1996.

Grant, R. G. *The Great Depression*. Barron's Educational Series, 2003.

McElmeel, Sharron L. *100 Most Popular Children's Authors*. Westport, CT: Teacher Ideas Press, 1999.

Rhoads, Emily. "Profile: Sid Fleischman." *Language Arts*, October 1989.

Senick, Gerard J. "(Albert) Sid(ney) Fleischman." *Children's Literature Review, Volume 15*. Detroit, MI: Gale Research Company.

Steinberg, Sybil S. "What Makes a Funny Children's Book? Five Writers Talk About Their Methods." *Publishers Weekly*, February 27, 1978.

Yolen, Jane. "Fleischman, (Albert) Sid (ney)." in Sara Pendergast and Tom Pendergast, eds., *St. James Guide to Children's Writers*. Detroit, MI: St. James Press, 1999.

Bibliography

Educational Paperback Association Web site. "Fleischman, Sid." Retrieved June 18, 2002 (www.edupaperback.org/pastbios/Fleischm.html).

Fleischman, Paul. "Sid Fleischman." *The Horn Book Magazine,* July–August 1987, pp. 429–432.

Fleischman, Sid. *The Abracadabra Kid: A Writer's Life*. New York: Greenwillow Books, 1996.

Fleischman, Sid. *Bandit's Moon*. New York: Bantam Doubleday Dell, 1998.

Fleischman, Sid. *By the Great Horn Spoon!* New York: Little, Brown, 1988.

Fleischman, Sid. *Chancy and the Grand Rascal*. New York: Atlantic Monthly Press, 1966.

Fleischman, Sid. *The Ghost in the Noonday Sun*. New York: Scholastic, 1991.

Fleischman, Sid. *The Ghost on Saturday Night*. New York: Beech Tree, 1997.

Fleischman, Sid. *Humbug Mountain*. New York: Atlantic-Little, Brown, 1998.

Fleischman, Sid. *Jim Ugly*. New York: Bantam Doubleday Dell, 1992.

Fleischman, Sid. *Jingo Django*. New York: Bantam Doubleday Dell, 1995.

Fleischman, Sid. *The Midnight Horse*. New York: Bantam Doubleday Dell, 1990.

Fleischman, Sid. *Mr. Mysterious & Company*. New York: Peach Tree Books, 1997.

Fleischman, Sid. "Newbery Medal Acceptance." *The Horn Book Magazine*, July–August 1987, pp. 442–451.

Fleischman, Sid. *The 13th Floor: A Ghost Story*. New York: Bantam Doubleday Dell, 1995.

Fleischman, Sid. *The Whipping Boy*. New York: Troll, 1987.

Hanf, Rich. "Welcome to the World of Dark Amusements . . . Specifically, Haunted Houses." FunSearch123.com Amusement E-MagazineTrade Edition. Retrieved September 1, 2002 (www.funsearch123.com/supplier/ezines/jul02.htm).

Bibliography

Mona Kerby's Author Corner. "Sid Fleischman." Retrieved July 11, 2002 (www.carr.lib.md.us/authco/fleischman.htm).

Mountain City Elementary Corner. "*The Whipping Boy*." Retrieved August 30, 2002 (www.mce.k12tn.net/reading8/whipping%5Fboy.htm).

Review of *Bandit's Moon*. *Publishers Weekly*, August 3, 1998, p. 86.

Shannon, David A. *The Great Depression*. New York: Prentice-Hall, 1960, pp. 1–11.

Sid Fleischman Web site. "Awards." Retrieved July 16, 2002 (http://www.sidfleischman.com).

Sid Fleischman Web site. "Biography." Retrieved July 16, 2002 (http://www.sidfleischman.com).

Sid Fleischman Web site. "Q and A." Retrieved July 16, 2002 (www.sidfleischman.com).

Senick, Gerard J., ed. "(Albert) Sid(ney) Fleischman." *Children's Literature Review, Volume 15*. Detroit, MI: Gale Research Company, 1988.

Steinberg, Sybil S. "What Makes a Funny Children's Book? Five Writers Talk About Their Methods." *Publishers Weekly*, February 27, 1978.

Teachers@random. "Sid Fleischman." Retrieved June 18, 2002 (www.randomhouse.com/teachers/authors/flei.html).

Yolen, Jane. "Fleischman, (Albert) Sid(ney)." Sara Pendergast and Tom Pendergast, ed. *St. James Guide to Children's Writers.* Detroit, MI: St. James Press, 1999, pp. 384–386.

Zvirin, Stephanie. Review of *Bo and Mzzz Mad*. *Booklist*, May 15, 2001, p. 1,750.

Source Notes

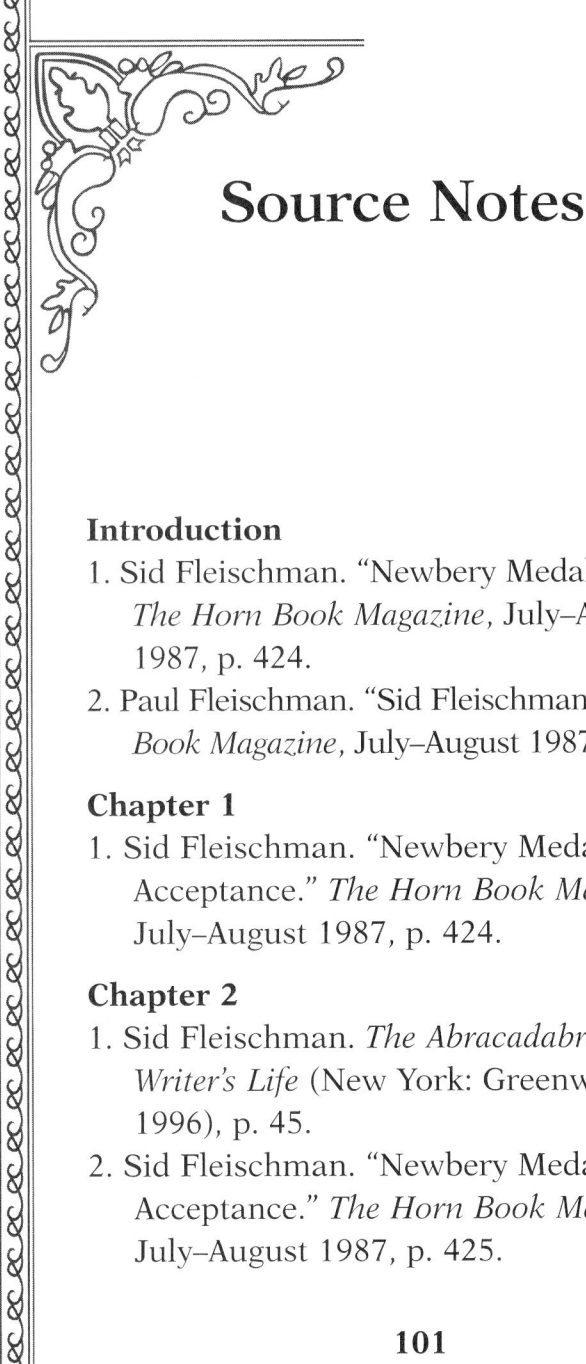

Introduction
1. Sid Fleischman. "Newbery Medal Acceptance." *The Horn Book Magazine*, July–August 1987, p. 424.
2. Paul Fleischman. "Sid Fleischman." *The Horn Book Magazine*, July–August 1987, pp. 429–430.

Chapter 1
1. Sid Fleischman. "Newbery Medal Acceptance." *The Horn Book Magazine*, July–August 1987, p. 424.

Chapter 2
1. Sid Fleischman. *The Abracadabra Kid: A Writer's Life* (New York: Greenwillow Press, 1996), p. 45.
2. Sid Fleischman. "Newbery Medal Acceptance." *The Horn Book Magazine*, July–August 1987, p. 425.

3. Sid Fleischman. *The Abracadabra Kid: A Writer's Life*, p. 72.
4. Ibid., p. 72.
5. Ibid., p. 80.
6. Ibid., p. 80.
7. Ibid., p. 83.

Chapter 3
1. Sid Fleischman. *The Abracadabra Kid: A Writer's Life* (New York: Greenwillow Books, 1996), p. 109.
2. Ibid., p. 120.
3. Ibid., p. 121.
4. Ibid., p. 126.
5. Ibid., p. 128.
6. Ibid., p. 114.
7. Ibid., p. 141.

Chapter 4
1. Sid Fleischman. "Newbery Medal Acceptance." *The Horn Book Magazine*, July–August 1987, p. 425.
2. Sid Fleischman. *The Abracadabra Kid: A Writer's Life* (New York: Greenwillow Books, 1996), p. 150.
3. Sid Fleischman. *Mr. Mysterious & Company* (New York: Peach Tree Books, 1997), pp. 96–97.
4. Dorothy M. Broderick. Review of *Mr. Mysterious & Company*. *New York Times Book Review*, May 13, 1962.
5. Sid Fleischman. "Newbery Medal Acceptance," p. 426.

Source Notes

6. Sid Fleischman. *The Abracadabra Kid: A Writer's Life*, pp. 157–158.
7. Sid Fleischman. *The Ghost on Saturday Night* (New York: Beech Tree, 1997), pp. 26–27.
8. Review of *Bandit's Moon. Publishers Weekly*, August 3, 1998, p. 86.

Chapter 5

1. Sid Fleischman. *The Abracadabra Kid: A Writer's Life* (New York: Greenwillow Books, 1996), p. 151.
2. Sid Fleischman. *The Ghost in the Noonday Sun* (New York: Scholastic, 1991), p. 6.
3. Sid Fleischman. *The Abracadabra Kid: A Writer's Life*, p. 164.
4. Sybil S. Steinberg. "What Makes a Funny Children's Book? Five Writers Talk About Their Methods." *Publishers Weekly*, February 27, 1978, p. 88.
5. Ibid., p. 88.
6. Charlotte S. Huck and Doris Young Kuhn. "Modern Fantasy and Humor: New Tall Tales." *Children's Literature in the Elementary School*, 2nd ed. (New York: Holt, Rinehart and Winston, 1968), pp. 337–338.
7. Sid Fleischman. *Chancy and the Grand Rascal* (New York: Greenwillow Books, 1966), p. 38.
8. Jane Yolen. Review of *Chancy and the Grand*

Rascal. New York Times Book Review, November 6, 1966, p. 40.
9. Sid Fleischman. *The Abracadabra Kid: A Writer's Life*, p. 171.
10. Ibid., p. 171.

Chapter 6
1. Sid Fleischman. "Newbery Medal Acceptance." *The Horn Book Magazine*, July–August 1987, p. 426.
2. Sid Fleischman. *The Whipping Boy* (New York: Troll, 1987), p. 72.
3. Sybil S. Steinberg. "What Makes a Funny Children's Book? Five Writers Talk About Their Methods." *Publishers Weekly*, February 27, 1978, p. 88.
4. Martha Saxton. Review of *The Whipping Boy. New York Times Book Review*, February 22, 1987, p. 23.
5. Jane Yolen. "Fleischman (Albert) Sid(ney)." Sara Pendergast and Tom Pendergast, eds. *St. James Guide to Children's Writers* (Detroit, MI: St. James Press, 1999), p. 386.

Chapter 7
1. Sid Fleischman Web site. "Biography." Retrieved July 16, 2002 (http://www.sidfleischman.com/biography.html).
2. Sid Fleischman Web site. "Biography."
3. Sid Fleischman. *The Abracadabra Kid: A Writer's Life* (New York: Greenwillow Books, 1996), p. 123.
4. Gerard J. Senick, ed. "(Albert) Sid(ney)

Source Notes

Fleischman." *Children's Review of Literature* (Detroit, MI: Gale Research Co., 1988), p. 104.
5. Sid Fleischman. "Newbery Medal Acceptance." *The Horn Book Magazine*, July–August 1987, p. 427.
6. Sid Fleischman. *The Abracadabra Kid: A Writer's Life* (New York: Greenwillow Books, 1996), p. 167.
7. Jane Yolen. "Fleischman (Albert) Sid(ney)." Sara Pendergast and Tom Pendergast, eds. *St. James Guide to Children's Writers* (Detroit, MI: St. James Press, 1999), p. 386.
8. Stephanie Zivrin. Review of *Bo and Mzzz Mad*. *Booklist*, May 15, 2001, p. 1,750.
9. Sid Fleischman Web site. "Biography."

Index

A
Abracadabra Day, 40
Abracadabra Kid: A Writer's Life, The, 44, 49–50, 63
Adams, John, 22
Alhambra, California, 18
American dream, 43–44
American Library Association's Library Service to Children, 58
Annyrose, 46
Atlantic Monthly Press, 38
atomic bombs, 26
Aunt Arabella, 42, 43
Aunt Katy, 49

B
Bacall, Lauren, 33
Badlands Kid, 37, 38, 39
Bandit's Moon, 46, 47
  characters in, 46–47
  plot of, 46–47

Between Cocktails, 17, 21
  writing of, 17–18
Big Dipper, 42
Blackberry, Ed, 64
Blood Alley, 27, 32, 33
  film of, 33
  plot of, 32
Bloodhound Gang, 55–56
Bloodhound Gang in the Case of Princess Tomorrow, The, 56
Bloodhound Gang in the Case of the Cackling Ghost, The, 55
Bloodhound Gang in the Case of the Flying Clock, The, 55
Bloodhound Gang in the Case of the Secret Message, The, 56
Bloodhound Gang in the Case of the 264 Pound Burglar, The, 56

Index

Bo & Mzzz Mad, 67
   characters in, 67, 68
   plot of, 67
Booklist, 67–68
Borneo, 26
Boston, Massachusetts, 42
Brando, Marlon, 39
Brooklyn, New York, 11
Brunei, 26
Brunner, William, 29
Buddy, 25
Bunyan, Paul, 52, 53
butler, 9, 43, 45
By the Great Horn Spoon!, 9, 42, 45
   characters in, 9, 42, 45
   plot of, 9, 42–44

C

California, 9, 12, 16, 17, 19, 40, 45, 53
California gold country, 17, 42, 43
California gold rush, 9, 43, 44, 46
Captain Scratch, 10, 49, 50—51
Carrol, Dick, 31
Chancy, 52, 53
Chancy and the Grand Rascal, 52, 53
   characters in, 52, 53, 54
   plot of, 52
Chandler, Raymond, 27
Chandu the Magician, 12–13
character development, 41

Children's Literature in the Elementary School, 52
China/Chinese, 27, 31, 32, 33, 44
civilian conservation camps, 16
Civil War, 52
Cold War, 32
Crookneck John, 20, 45, 46

D

Deadly Companions, The, 39
dialect, 20, 66
Disappearing Act, 66
   characters in, 66
   plot of, 66–67

E

Egyptian Box illusion, 37, 38
Emerald Bay Camp, 16
England, 11

F

Fait, Charles W., 14
Fawcett Publications, 31
Finch, Oliver, 10, 49, 50
Flagg, Jack, 42–43
Fleischman, Anne, 33
Fleischman, Betty Taylor, 22, 25, 27, 31, 32, 33, 35
Fleischman, Honey, 12, 14
Fleischman, Jane, 31, 35–36, 40
Fleischman, Paul, 8, 32
Fleischman, Pearl, 12, 14
Fleischman, Reuben, 11, 12

Fleischman, Sid
  autobiography, 19–20, 44, 49–50, 63
  being a writer, 7, 10, 17, 27, 62–68
  children of, 8, 31, 32, 33, 40
  and dialect/speech, 20, 66
  and education, 14, 18, 21, 22, 29
  first book, 7–8, 17–18, 21
  first children's book, 8, 35–37, 48
  and libraries, 13, 22
  and magic, 7, 10, 12–13, 14–15, 16–20, 21, 22, 64
  main characters of, 9, 10
  in the military, 24–27
  mother of, 11, 21
  Newbery Medal speech, 7, 13, 35, 57
  as a newspaperman, 29–30, 31, 41
  and research, 44, 63–64
  as a screenwriter, 33–34, 36, 59
  settings of stories, 8–9
  and ships, 25
  sisters of, 11–12, 14
  tips for young writers, 65–66
  using experience in writing, 20, 27, 31, 32, 40–42, 45
  writing detective stories, 27, 59
  and writing process, 28, 62, 63, 64–66
  working for a spook show, 19–21
  writing short stories, 21, 25, 27, 29
  youth of, 7–8, 11–15, 16–23
Francisco Spook and Magic, 19, 20, 21

G

Gamage, Bo, 67, 68
Ghost in the Noonday Sun, The, 10, 49, 51
  characters in, 10, 25, 49–50
  plot of, 10, 50
Ghost on Saturday Night, The, 20, 45
  characters in, 20, 50
  plot of, 45
Gold Medal Book, 31, 32
Grand Rascal, 52, 53, 54
Great Depression, 13, 16, 19

H

Hackett family, 37, 39, 40, 41, 64
Hippodrome Theater, 19
Hiroshima, Japan, 26
historic settings, 8–9, 10, 25, 56, 57, 67
Hold-Your-Nose Billy, 9, 59, 60
Hollywood, California, 36, 39
Hongkew, 32, 33
Horace/Prince Brat, 58, 60, 61
Humbug Mountain, 41

108

Index

humor in stories, 9, 48–50, 51, 59–60, 61

I
immigrants, 11

J
Japanese/Japan, 22, 23, 24, 26, 33
Jemmy, 58–59
Jewish refugees, 32, 33
Jim Ugly, 41
Jingo Django, 50
Jones, Heck, 54
Judge Wigglesforth, 10, 50

K
Kinne, Fred, 30

L
Leyte Gulf, 26
Liberty, 25
library, 13, 22, 40
Lithuania, 11
Little Shop of Hocus Pocus, 21
Look Behind You, Lady, 31—32
Los Angeles, California, 18, 19

M
Macao, 32
magic, 7, 10, 13, 18, 22
magic show, 8, 14, 15, 17, 37, 41
magic tricks, 13, 14, 15, 17, 18, 21, 37, 38
magician, 7, 10, 13, 14, 17, 31, 37, 45, 64
Magicians' Club of San Diego, 14

Man Who Died Laughing, The, 31
main characters, role of, 9, 37, 41
Martinka, Aunt Juna, 67
Martinka, Charles, 67
Martinka, Madeleine (Mzzz Mad), 67, 68
McBroom, Farmer Josh, 10, 54, 55
McBroom tall tales, 20
McBroom Tells the Truth, 54
McBroom's Ghost, 55
   plot of, 55
McBroom's Wonderful One-Acre Farm, 10
   characters in, 10
   plot of, 10
merchant marine captain, 32
Midnight Horse, The, 10
   characters in, 10
   plot of, 10
Midwest, 8, 14, 20, 52, 53
Mirthful Conjurers, 14–15
Mr. Mysterious & Company, 8, 35, 36, 37, 39–40, 41, 42, 48, 64
   characters in, 37, 38, 64
   inspiration for, 35
   plot of, 37
Mrs. Daggatt, 50
Murieta, Joaquin, 47

N
Nagasaki, Japan, 26
names, unusual, 45
Nantucket, Massachusetts, 25

naval reserve, 24
Nazis, 32
Newbery Medal, 7, 8, 13, 32, 35, 57, 58
New England, 8–9, 10
New York, 11, 12
New York Times Book Review, 39, 60
Norfolk, Virginia, 25

O

Old West, 8, 36
O. O. Mary, 46

P

Pacific Fleet, 26
Pearl (Sid's aunt), 18
Pearl Harbor, Hawaii, 22, 24
Philippines, 26
Phoenix Press, 28, 29
Pilgrims, 10
pirates, 10, 25, 49, 50
Point, 30, 31
Politi, Leo, 35, 40
Praiseworthy, 9, 43, 45
Professor Pepper, 20, 45, 46, 50
Publishers Weekly, 47
pulp magazines, 29

R

radio, 12
Roosevelt, Franklin D., 16
Russia, 11
Ryan, Buddy, 14, 15, 16, 19, 42
Ryan, Mary, 14, 15

S

sailors, 25
Samar Bay, 26
Sam (Sid's uncle), 17, 18
San Diego, California, 12, 14, 18, 21, 27, 37
San Diego Daily Journal, 29–30, 31
San Diego State College, 21–22, 29
San Fernando Valley, 45
San Francisco, California, 43, 44
Santa Monica, California, 34, 62
Santa Monica Public Library, 35, 40
screenwriters' strike, 34, 36, 39
See'n Is Believ'n, 16
Sellers, Peter, 51
Shanghai, China, 27, 31, 32
Shanghai Flame, 31
ships, 25, 43
short stories, 21, 25, 27
Sierra Nevada, 16, 42
sleight of hand, 8, 13, 15
sleight of mind, 51, 64
South China Sea, 26, 32
spook show, 19, 20, 21, 45
Straw Donkey Case, The, 28
sweatshops, 12

T

Tahoe, Lake, 15
tailors, 12, 18
Taiwan (Formosa), 32

Index

tall tales, 20, 51–52, 53, 54, 55
13th Floor: A Ghost Story, The, 8, 10, 25
   characters in, 10, 25, 51
Tijuana, Mexico, 28
Touch, 10

U
United States, 11, 13, 18, 40
   government, 16, 29, 32
   in World War II, 23, 24, 25, 26
USS *Albert T. Harris*, 25, 26, 27
U.S.S.R., 32

V
Van Deerlin, Lionel, 30
vaudeville, 8, 18

Venice, California, 66–67
villains, comic, 48, 49, 50, 51, 64

W
Wayne, John, 33
Wellman, Bill, 33
Westerns, 36, 39, 67
Whipping Boy, The, 7, 9, 57–61
   characters in, 9, 58, 59, 60, 61
women's right to vote, 12
World War II, 18, 23, 24–27, 32

Y
Yellowleg, 34, 36, 39
Yolen, Jane, 53–54, 61

About the Author

Jeri Freedman has a B.A. from Harvard University and spent fifteen years working in companies in the biomedical and high-technology fields. She is the author of several plays and, under the name Foxxe, is the coauthor of two science fiction novels. She lives in Boston.

Photo Credits

Cover, p. 2 Rhonda Williams.

Design: Tahara Hasan; Editor: Annie Sommers